Published by Hachette Partworks Ltd.
ISBN: 978-1-908648-62-4
Date of Printing: March 2013
Printed in Malaysia by Tien Wah Press

Tinker Bell and the Lost Treasure

It was autumn in Pixie Hollow. The fairies had been busy harvesting pixie dust, which was essential to them – without it, they couldn't change the seasons or do any special magic.

At the end of harvest, Tinker Bell was summoned to see Queen Clarion, the Minister for Autumn and Fairy Mary.

The minister explained that this year, the Autumn Revelry would coincide with a blue harvest moon. A new sceptre had to be created for the occasion – and Tinker Bell had been chosen for the job!

"At the top of the sceptre, you will place a moonstone," said the minister. "When the blue moon is at its peak, its rays will pass through the gem, creating blue pixie dust. The blue dust restores the Pixie Dust Tree!"

When Tinker Bell told Terence that she was going to make the new sceptre, he wanted to help.

"I can collect supplies for you and give you advice," he offered.

The next morning, Terence arrived bright and early to start work with Tink. And over the next few days, it seemed that every time Tink looked up, there was Terence, ready to help.

Tinker Bell began to find Terence a bit irritating. He was always offering advice – whether she needed it or not!

Terence meant well, but he was distracting her. She needed to focus on her task to design and make the finest sceptre ever created.

At last, it was time for Tink to fit the moonstone onto the top of her sceptre.

"Steady, this is the tricky part," warned Terence.

"I know!" said Tinker Bell.

"You've got to match the trajectory of the light beam with the..."

"Shh! Would you please!" snapped Tink.

As Tinker Bell placed the moonstone into its setting, a piece of the sceptre broke off. Terence offered to go out and find a sharp tool so she could fix the piece back on.

"I'll be right back," promised Terence.

"Take your time," muttered Tink.

Soon, Terence was back with a compass, which wasn't sharp at all! Impatiently, Tink pushed the compass. It rolled away, landing on top of the sceptre and breaking it!

"This is your fault!" Tink shouted at Terence.

"Fine! Last time I try to help you!" Terence yelled back, as he stomped out.

Tinker Bell was so angry that she kicked the compass. Its lid sprang open... and landed on the moonstone, which shattered into pieces.

Tink needed help! She went to see Fairy Mary, who was at the theatre. Tink couldn't bring herself to admit what she had done, so she tactfully asked Mary where she could find a new moonstone. Fairy Mary shook her head. There was only one moonstone, she explained, and without it, things would be pretty tough in Pixie Hollow.

THUMP! It was too much for Tink and she fainted.

The show began. The storytelling fairy told the tale of the Mirror of Incanta. Long ago, in Never Land, some pirates had found the mirror. It had the power to grant three wishes, but the pirates had only used two of them before their ship was wrecked and the mirror, with one last wish still to grant, disappeared. The only clue to its whereabouts was a riddle, which began:

Journey due north, past Never Land,
Where a far away island is close at hand,
When you're alone but not alone.
You will find help in an arch of stone.

Tink decided she had to find the mirror and use its last wish to repair the moonstone. But she didn't have enough pixie dust for the trip, so she went to ask Terence to give her some more.

Terence was still angry with Tinker Bell and didn't feel like helping her. He reminded her of the rules. Each fairy was allowed only one ration of pixie dust.

"I'm on my own, then," said Tink, sadly.

Pixie dust or no pixie dust, Tinker Bell had to find that mirror. She built herself a balloon and packed everything she needed for her expedition. When everything was ready for take-off, she sprinkled the balloon with some dust and gently, the balloon began to rise. The voyage had begun!

Night fell, and as the balloon drifted across the starry sky, Tinker Bell felt hungry. She opened her bag, but all her boysenberry rolls and pumpernickel muffins were gone. The only thing left in the bag was a guilty-looking firefly!

"Out! Shoo!" shouted Tink. But the firefly stayed put.

Tink peered at her map, but it was too dark to see properly. Luckily, the firefly, who was called Blaze, came to the rescue. His glowing body was like a miniature lamp!

"OK, you can stay – for now," said Tinker Bell.

The next morning, Tink and Blaze woke up with a start when the balloon got stuck in a tree.

"This must be the lost island," cried Tink. "And there's the stone arch from the story! You stay here and guard the balloon. I'll be right back."

Tinker Bell flew to the arch, but when she got there, it turned out to be two intertwined trees. Then she noticed the balloon. It had got loose from the tree and was drifting away!

Tinker Bell was in despair.

"I've lost my balloon, I've lost my pixie dust and I'm starving. What have I done?" she said to Blaze.

Blaze was determined to help. He called up his insect friends and, together, they brought Tink food and drink. Then they led her to the stone arch she had been searching for.

After they found the arch, Tinker Bell and Blaze reached a bridge, guarded by two fierce trolls.

"Beat it, before we grind your bones to make our bed!" snarled one of the trolls.

"You mean BREAD, you knucklehead, not bed!" said the other.

The two trolls began to argue. In fact, they were so busy arguing that they didn't notice Tinker Bell and Blaze sneaking past them.

At last, the two friends arrived at the shore of the island. And there, on the beach, was a huge, old shipwreck – just as the riddle had foretold.

"Let's go!" said Tinker Bell.

Nervously, the pair crept into the wreck in search of the magic mirror. Inside the ship, it was dark, damp and very creaky. Tinker Bell shivered with cold and fear.

In the captain's cabin, the two friends found a haul of fabulous treasure, and there, amidst the jewels and coins, was the Mirror of Incanta!

"OK. Deep breath. I wish..." began Tinker Bell, but Blaze was putting her off by buzzing in her ear.

"I wish..." she began again, but Blaze was still buzzing around her.

"I wish... Blaze, I wish you'd be quiet for one minute!" she cried.

All of a sudden, the buzzing stopped.

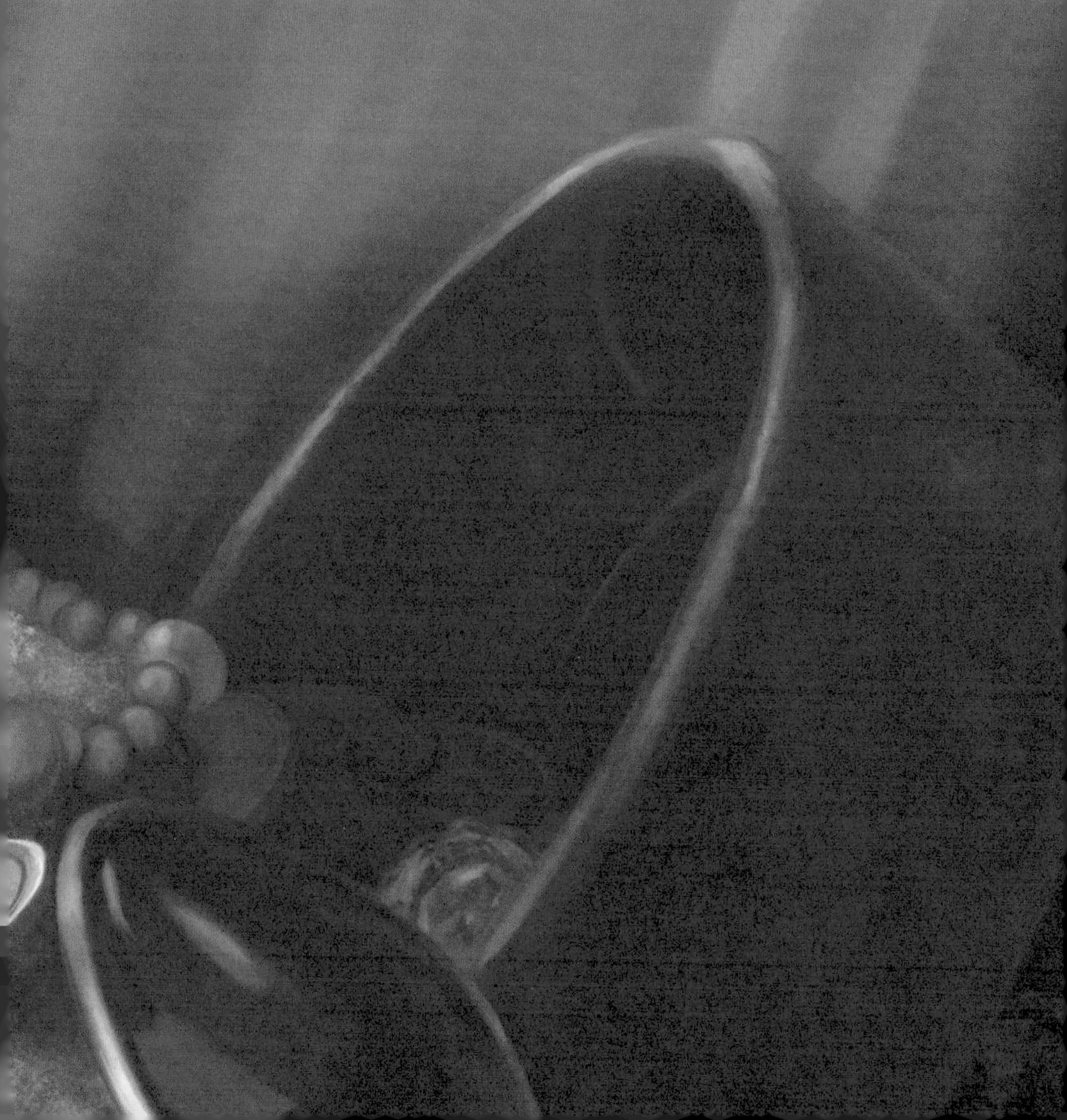

Tinker Bell was furious that she had wasted her only wish.

"It's all your fault!" she yelled at Blaze. Then she realised that she was blaming Blaze unfairly, just as she had blamed Terence. Just then, Terence's face appeared in the mirror.

"Terence, I'm so sorry," said Tink. "I wish you were here."

"But I am here!" Terence replied. He had found Tink's notes and designs, guessed what her plans were and followed her to the island.

Tink was overjoyed to see her friend.

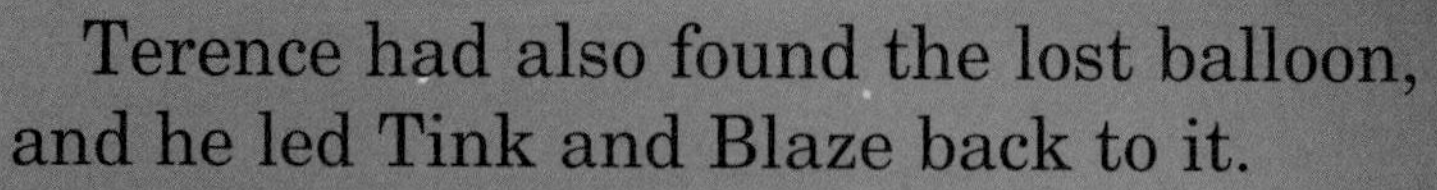

Terence had also found the lost balloon, and he led Tink and Blaze back to it.

"I don't know if it will help, but I brought this," said Terence, handing Tink the broken sceptre.

"Hey, I've got an idea!" said Tink. Together, they worked all night to repair the sceptre, as the blue moon rose in the sky.

Back home, the Autumn Revelry was just about to start when the three friends arrived.

"Fairies of Pixie Hollow," announced Tinker Bell, "I present... the Autumn Sceptre!"

The crowd gasped when Tink unveiled the strange sceptre, made from moonstone fragments, bits of the old sceptre and the magic mirror's frame.

"Please work!" whispered Tink.

The rays from the blue moon reached the sceptre. As the moonbeams reflected off all the miniature moonstones, everyone held their breath. And then, in the next instant, the air was filled with clouds and clouds of magical, blue pixie dust – more dust than anyone had ever seen!

Everyone congratulated Tinker Bell on her clever invention. But she knew that she could never, ever have done it without her friends.